The Witch's Hat

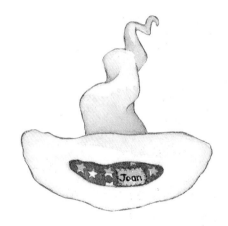

Written by Jane Mackay

Illustrated by Claire Pound

2

3

8

Fresh Cream Cakes

Village Bakery

Bread & Rolls

Birthday cakes made to order

Fresh filled rolls and pasties

PETER

Bread freshly Baked Today

10

CROWN AND ANCHOR

Please use other door →

BAR

HATS & CO

LITTER